MONTANA PROTECTOR

HEIRS OF GUARDIAN VALLEY

BOOK ONE

HALLIE BENNETT

I0619585

Searching for more protective heroes?
Check out the Mountain Men of
Suitor's Crossing series <u>here</u>[1]!

---

1. https://www.amazon.com/Protected-Mountain-Man-
Romance-Crossing-ebook/dp/B0BNM2M6RY

CHAPTER ONE

HEATH MANNING

"You're already dark and broody like the Grim Reaper."

THE PROBLEM WITH BEING a small-town institution is that everybody always knows your business. Like the fact that my dad fucked us over by bankrupting our family's ranch—one that had been part of Guardian Valley's history since the town's founding over a century ago.

But instead of extending our family's legacy, Dad's inability to adjust to changing times cut it short. The ranch lost money hand over fist until he was forced to sell it himself rather than let the bank auction it off in parcels. He sold our family's home to some billionaire CEO I'd never heard of and who I now worked for—as an employee rather than the ranch's owner.

Talk about a hell of a welcome home after a career in the Marines.

"I was sorry to hear about your father, Heath," Mr. Jones says, invading my dark corner at the community center.

Guardian Valley is hosting its annual Fall Harvest Dance tonight. A popular event that draws everyone within the surrounding area. It's our last hurrah before the freezing grip of winter grabs us by the balls and makes life miserable.

"Thanks." One word and I take a sip of my scotch.

I've only been back in town for a month. A month since I found out my dad sold the ranch. Three weeks since he died from a freak car accident. Honestly, I should have skipped out on the dance, using grief as an excuse, but my sister wanted to come. To take comfort with her friends.

I figured it might be a nice break from my days filled with getting the ranch back on its feet after Mr. Billionaire CEO's influx of cash. A mystery billionaire CEO whom I'll never meet because the wily Mr. Foster apparently had his own mortality breathing down his neck, passing away two weeks ago.

It hadn't made sense to me why the old man would buy a ranch when death was knocking on his door.

Until a lawyer appeared with Mr. Foster's will which stated that a group of strangers would be arriving at the ranch soon, and the first stranger would be the lucky recipient of the Serenity Ranch deed.

My hand tightens on the glass tumbler at the reminder.

Yeah, Dad really fucked us over.

He knew my retirement was near. That I was coming home for good. I don't know how I could've saved the ranch from the mountain of debt it was under, but he should've given me a chance to do *something* before selling off a family legacy that rightfully belonged to me and Samantha.

"Well, I'll just be on my way then." Mr. Jones must read the scowl of frustration on my face because he smartly shuffles away with a wave of goodbye.

I'm being an asshole, sequestering myself to this shadowy corner rather than making the rounds through old neighbors and family friends. But there's only so much a man can take of condolences and curiosity.

Everybody's awfully sorry about the loss of my dad, and everyone is equally interested in the future of the ranch.

Neither of those things are topics I want to delve into with anyone outside of my sister. Hell, even she and I have avoided discussing it too deeply, content with sticking to our roles. Me handling the physical ranch labor needed outside while she manages the main house and the surrounding cabins.

"Scare another one off?" Speaking of the devil, Samantha sidles up beside me to bump my shoulder with hers—a feat considering our height difference.

"I don't know what you're talking about."

"I'm talking about you dismissing every Guardian Valley citizen who comes to say hello."

"I warned you I wouldn't be good company tonight, so technically this is your fault if anybody's feathers are ruffled by my attitude."

Samantha hums in her throat before grabbing my half-empty glass and downing the rest of the amber liquid.

"Hey!"

"You don't need any more of this," she lifts the empty glass, "You're already dark and broody like the Grim Reaper. You don't need to add more alcohol to the mix."

"Thanks, *mother*."

"You're welcome." Samantha winks and gives me a three-finger wave before turning on her heel, setting my glass on an empty table, and rejoining the dancers two-stepping at the center of the building.

She's right.

I don't need to be downing tumblers of whiskey like they're bottles of water in the middle of the desert, especially since I still have a twenty-minute drive out to the ranch after this. But if I don't have something to do with my hands—like holding a drink—then this urge to leave may finally win. Because standing here alone, besieged by happy people, with nothing to do but watch them flirt and dance isn't my idea of fun.

Screw it.

I'll head outside for some fresh air and text Samantha to see if she needs me to stay to give her a ride home or if one of her friends will do it. Maybe a lungful of brisk Montana air will settle some of the tension I've been carrying.

Not that it's worked in the past month since I stepped onto the tarmac after officially retiring from the Marine Corps. But perhaps, for once, life will be kind to me.

No career.

No ranch.

No father.

Each gone in quick succession.

Yeah, I doubt life gives a shit about me at all.

CHAPTER TWO

ADELINE CROUP

"...a lone lawman taming this rugged land with only his bare hands and wit."

WELCOMING LIGHT SPILLS from the windows of Guardian Valley's community center. The street is packed with cars, a fact I learned the hard way when I had to circle the block three times before accepting my misfortune and parking a couple buildings over.

At least it's not freezing cold.

The autumn breeze is chilly but not unbearable, and with the state of my nerves right now, I could use the invigorating wash of wind to evaporate the sweat coating my skin.

Another local shop's cute decor piques my interest as I stop to appreciate the floating red and orange leaves hung with nearly-invisible fishing wire. Guardian Valley is charming, quaint. A small town nestled between two mountains and my new home.

For a year.

Unless I decide to stay longer.

But a year was what Mr. Dell Foster's will required, so that's what I'm going to do.

I never met Mr. Foster. Had a vague memory of seeing him once after the disastrous plane crash that killed my mom, along with nine other passengers. Truthfully, I avoid thinking about that part of my childhood at all, but one phone call from Mr. Foster's attorney changed things.

Because the old man left his vast fortune to me and the four other kids orphaned by the plane crash.

Of course, despite the generosity, he hadn't made it a simple exchange of checks. No, he'd outlined one particular requirement.

None of us could access our inheritance until we followed one condition: *You must reside in Guardian Valley for a term of twelve months before receiving your share of the inheritance in full.*

The only portion not withheld is Serenity Ranch. It'll provide us with a place to stay while waiting for the year to expire. Waiting for *what* exactly, I have no clue. It doesn't make much sense to me, but who am I to argue with a dead billionaire's guilty conscience?

Stuffing my hands in the pockets of my jacket, my steps slow the closer I get to the community center. I don't know why I thought it'd be a good idea to attend something like this. A Fall Harvest Dance. It's meant for friends and family—a close-knit community.

Not a stranger forced to move here to receive a surprise inheritance.

But when I'd driven by the huge banner hanging across Main Street earlier, the thought of checking out a local community dance sounded fun. Sounded like the kind of thing the woman I wanted to be would do.

Because the current me? Didn't love her life. Cringed at how much time she's wasted hiding away in her comfortable bubble.

After my mom died when I was nine, Gran took me into her tiny two-bedroom apartment in a complex predominantly made up of retirees. She raised me as best she could between episodes of Jeopardy! and Wheel of Fortune, but the outcome was a little girl who'd transformed into a miniature seventy-year old by the time Gran's health started to decline.

At sixteen and seventy-one, our roles reversed.

So rather than going to football games or homecoming dances, I stayed home. Partially due to my crippling shyness and fear of socializing with people my own age, but also because Gran needed me.

It was easy enough to ignore my shortcomings while I tended to her, but now Gran's gone. Five years ago this past July. And instead of exploring the world like the average woman in her twenties, I settled into Gran's life, entrenched myself in the cozy comfort of woolen sweaters and daytime television.

I got an online bachelor's degree and found a remote job that allowed me to easily sequester myself to Gran's old recliner, watching our favorite shows while working on my laptop. It's a simple but lonely life, especially when the only one shouting answers to the final clue on Jeopardy! is me.

I want a husband, kids, friends—a family.

The problem with those things is they require me to actually leave the house. First to find a man who could overlook my shy awkwardness enough to fall in love and want children with me, and second to figure out how adults even make friends at the age of twenty-nine.

Sure, chatting with geriatrics at the senior center had been easy enough when Gran was a buffer. But now I'm on my own.

"You can do this," I mutter aloud, trying to hype myself up enough to enter the dance across the street and mingle with the townspeople of Guardian Valley.

Because fate isn't going to drop my dream husband into my lap.

Trust me, I've tried to believe it could happen with every attractive delivery man or guy I ran into at the grocery store, but life doesn't work like that. It doesn't favor quiet women too afraid to initiate conversations or look men in the eyes.

But the inheritance letter that arrived in the mail a week ago heralded a major change for my future. It was the kick I needed to conquer my shyness and grab hold of the kind of life I've always dreamed of.

Or so I hoped.

It already had me moving across the country, leaving behind the only home I've known for the last two decades.

Taking a deep breath, I cross the street and head for the double doors open to everyone inclined to join the fun inside. I keep my gaze forward, considering my options for what to do once I'm actually in the building.

Should I grab a drink and linger at the edges of the crowd in the hopes someone will take pity on me?

No, that sounds pathetic.

I can't expect a better life by repeating the same mistakes—being a wallflower who's afraid to speak with strangers.

A large figure blocks the glow of light emanating through the doorway. The stranger is silhouetted in black before exiting onto the sidewalk. Worn boots lead to dark jeans, a black button-down shirt, and a cowboy hat.

Whoa.

The man looks like he popped straight from one of the 1950s Westerns Gran loved, and immediately, my imagination goes wild with thoughts of a lone lawman taming this rugged land with only his bare hands and wit.

God, you really are desperate for a man.

However, fate reminds me why dangerously attractive men like him are not for the likes of me, because the toe of my shoe snags on the curb of the sidewalk, casting me forward with a harsh momentum that almost seems vindictive.

I struggle to remove my hands from my pockets in time to catch myself, and the jarring impact radiates from my palms to my locked elbows before I crumple to the ground with a yelp. My knees burn where they scraped across the concrete, and I curse my decision to wear a dress, even though it's calf-length with a layer of tights underneath the skirt. It's obvious they never stood a chance against the rough pavement.

Tears of pain threaten to fall as my lungs inflate with shaky breaths. My first attempt to be brave, and this is what happens?

In front of a gorgeous cowboy to boot?

Maybe I'm not meant for a different life after all. Because what good does an inheritance do if I'm still the same old awkward Adeline?

CHAPTER THREE

HEATH

"That's my girl."

I'M A DECENT-LOOKING guy.

Had my fair share of women over the past forty-two years, so I know I'm not the ugliest mug around. But I've never had a woman literally throw herself at me.

Except for this one.

One minute I'm leaving the dance and heading toward my truck, since Samantha said she'd catch a ride with Jasmine, and the next moment, a pretty blonde is falling at my feet.

"Are you alright?" I kneel on the ground and gently help the woman roll to her side. She's young, her innocent face pale from shock. Blood stains the concrete as well as her palms and knees—marring the fragile skin—and a wave of protectiveness slams into me at the sight. "Damn, you really did a number on yourself, didn't you?"

"Not... on... purpose," she gasps out. The stuttered words are clearly painful to spit out as she fights to catch her breath. Her chest rises and falls too quickly, and instinctively, I place my palm over her heart and allow the slightest pressure of my weight.

"Easy now. You're going to be alright. Just breathe with me, okay?" I press a little more on the deep valley between her breasts, hoping the heaviness helps to calm her nervous system. Like a modified weighted blanket.

Our breaths synchronize as she keeps her brown gaze locked with mine, until finally—*finally*—I feel the rhythm of her heartbeat begin to slow, returning to normal.

"Good girl," I murmur before glancing back towards the dance, debating my options. She needs a first aid kit, but do I really want the attention that would rain down upon us if I return to the dance with a wounded mystery woman in my arms?

Hell no.

"Come on, I've got a first aid kit in my truck."

"No... that's okay." She attempts a wobbly smile and slowly rises to a sitting position. "I'm... fine."

"Don't be stubborn. You're bleeding all over the sidewalk," I argue, my mind made up. I don't like seeing her injured, and I'll like it even less if there's an audience to her pain. "My truck isn't too far. I'll have you patched up in no time."

Not giving her time to protest, I slide my arms beneath her legs and back before lifting her up to my chest, standing with the momentum.

"What... What are you... Put me down! I'm too heavy!" Panic tinges her voice as she begins wiggling in my arms. An elbow digs into my gut, and I grunt at the impact.

"Shh... You're safe, trust me." My tone lowers to the calming one I use for horses on the ranch since she's as skittish as a newborn colt. "It'll hurt like a bitch if you try walking, and I'm not about to let you hurt yourself some more."

Anxious eyes meet mine. They're huge behind her crooked glasses, most likely jostled from her fall. We stand that way—quiet, contemplative, *stubborn*—with her secure in my arms, both of us studying the other.

She's a soft, comforting handful, and I squeeze her closer to my chest. A quilted jacket hides the shape of her body, but the fleshy give of her thighs promises a delicious curvy treat beneath the puffy outer layer.

She's too young for you, asshole.

"Are we good, baby?" The endearment slips without warning out of my mouth. Feels right, despite her being a stranger. Despite the obvious age difference.

Which is at least a decade, if not more. Because I've got silver-flecked hair and weathered skin from being stationed under the desert sun for years while she's fresh and innocent, practically glowing with vitality under the harvest moon.

When she nods that she's fine, that she'll let me carry her, relief pours through my veins because I don't have to let her go yet. I can give in to this need to protect her. To ensure her safety, even from a few scrapes and bruises.

My long strides eat up the sidewalk once she settles into my embrace, though her muscles remain stiff beneath my hands. At my truck, I carefully set her down in the passenger's seat before reaching into the back of the cab for the first aid kit.

Its main purpose is for ranch accidents, but it comes in handy for the random mishap, too.

She hisses in discomfort as I dab an alcohol wipe across her knee. "Sorry, I know it stings." My movements gentle even more as I bend to blow over the scrape, praying it'll dampen the pain. "I'm Heath, by the way. Are you visiting for the dance?"

"No," she says quietly.

"Just moved to town?"

"Yes... Sort of..." Her nose scrunches as she flounders, her lips rolling inward. Trembling fingers fix her glasses, pushing them higher on her pert nose, and the nervous gesture is oddly endearing.

"How do you *sort of* move somewhere?" I tease, offering an encouraging smile. One that will hopefully relax the tenseness radiating from her body.

"Tomorrow's the official move-in day. I just got into town this afternoon."

"Wow, I'm surprised you have the energy to attend a dance after traveling." Unless she isn't coming from very far.

Of course, I would've taken *any* excuse to avoid tonight's festivities, even the twenty-minute drive from the ranch, if not for Samantha.

Although if my mystery girl did live close, we probably would have met before now.

Granted, I've been a career military man for the past twenty years, so it's not like I'm current with the town gossip and the surrounding counties' residents. But I've been back enough times throughout the years to not be totally clueless. And since Guardian Valley offers the best amenities within a ninety-mile radius, it's not unheard of that we would've met.

"Probably wasn't my best idea." She tucks her chin into her chest and shrugs. Like she's trying to make herself smaller out of shame.

"Hey." I cup her cheek and tilt her head up. "You're a pretty girl who wanted to dance. Nothing wrong with that. Just look out for curbs next time, yeah?"

A pink flush warms my palm as she whispers, "Yeah."

"That's my girl." And damn if I don't feel the truth of her being mine down to my bones.

God, I'm fucked.

Because not only am I too old and jaded for someone as sweet as her, but I've got nothing to offer a woman.

The family ranch doesn't belong to me anymore.

Strangers own it.

The only thing I have is one of the ranch cabins available to employees. Who knows if the new owners will want to keep me around to run things when they arrive?

I could be homeless *and* jobless soon.

And no woman wants that.

CHAPTER FOUR

ADELINE

"...he could have any woman he wanted quicker than a bull rider's eight seconds."

THAT'S MY GIRL.

That's. My. Girl.

The words spin around in my head—along with the other sweet things Heath's said—making me dizzy with yearning.

He probably didn't mean anything by his comments, but I've never belonged to anyone, never felt so protected. And the thought of being his, *Heath's girl*, sends a shiver of desire down my body, my stomach clenching with nervous energy. My knees and palms still throb from tripping, but there's a different ache settling between my thighs.

One that's as unexpected as it is welcomed.

Because I'm still a virgin.

Technically, the only orgasms I've experienced have been self-given. And while Heath seems like the type of man to know how to treat a woman—*in and out of bed*—my shyness hasn't magically disappeared. Evidenced by the one word answers I've given him.

How exactly do I expect to go from shy virgin to a one night stand? I must be out of my mind!

Even if I never felt safer than when I was in his strong arms, it doesn't mean we're soul mates.

A random memory surfaces at the thought. Gran had a friend who lived in a town called Suitor's Crossing where they believed in soul mates. Gave them a special name and everything: *heart sparks*.

That's not what this is.

A one-time fling is all it would be. There's no way Heath would want something more with a woman like me who's too shy and too plump. I'm sure he could have any woman he wanted quicker than a bull rider's eight seconds.

Someone beautiful and confident. Someone with a sexy name like Vanessa or Alessandra. Not an old-fashioned name like mine.

Gracious! I haven't even told him my name, yet here I am fantasizing about belonging to him.

"Adeline," I blurt out.

"What was that?"

"Adeline, that's my name." I try ducking my head again as embarrassment engulfs me in a hot flush, but his large hand holds my cheek in place, not allowing me to hide from his deep blue gaze.

"Adeline..."

I shiver. Maybe my name's sexy, after all, at least when it's spoken in Heath's gravelly tone.

"It suits you. Do you ever go by Addie?"

"Sometimes. Depends on the person." Truthfully, only one person has ever called me Addie, and that was my mom. I never got close enough to other people for them to feel comfortable with a shortened moniker.

And Gran hated abbreviated versions of names.

If you're going to call a child Addie, then you might as well have written it on the birth certificate. Hers says 'Adeline.' That's her name, so that's what I'm going to use.

I still remember that conversation. It was right before the plane crash when Mom had dropped me off so Gran could look after me while she was gone.

"Addie it is, then." He grins and swipes his thumb over my bottom lip before directing his attention back to my injuries. I sit there in a daze while he quickly tends to my scratches, the fatigue from my earlier drive starting to settle over me.

I tried to cut the trip from Kansas City to Guardian Valley into manageable pieces. Driving six hours the first day. Then another six to Deadwood, South Dakota because I couldn't *not* stop to visit the infamous town, especially with Gran's love of Westerns instilled in me from a young age.

The history of the city was captivating, but loneliness crept up during the museum tours since everyone else was traveling with family. Exploring solo sounded amazing based on social media accounts I'd seen, but the reality wasn't for me.

I'm already used to being by myself twenty-four-seven, and having the glaring hole of emptiness in my life thrown in my face because I didn't have anyone to share the experience with was disheartening.

"All finished, Sleeping Beauty."

I jerk to an upright position after nodding off against the passenger side headrest. Using the tips of my fingers, since my palm is lightly wrapped in gauze, I straighten my glasses and scoot closer to the edge of the seat, preparing for the impact of jumping to the street from this height.

"Thank you. I'm sorry I ruined the dance for you."

What if he has a date waiting for him back at the community center? What if he only stepped out for some fresh air, then I waylaid him with my clumsiness?

Oh, God. This whole time I've been imagining what it'd be like to belong to a man like him. Not a man *like* him. *Him. Heath.* And he could have a wife or girlfriend worrying about him at the dance.

A second-wind breathes new life into my weary body at the humiliating prospect, and I hurry to scramble down from the truck and out of Heath's life.

It stings when I grab the side of the open door, but there's nothing for it now. I've got to get out of here.

"Hang on there. You didn't ruin anything, baby. I was heading home for the night." His hands grip my waist to stop my frantic movements. "Before you go rushing off, are you sure it's safe for you to drive? You almost fell asleep just a minute ago."

CHAPTER FIVE

HEATH

"You're too fucking old for a sweet little thing like her."

ADELINE ACTS LIKE THE hounds of hell are nipping at her heels as she tries hopping down from the truck. I don't know what happened to morph the contented sleepy look on her face to frenzied panic, but I'm sure as hell going to find out.

"The hotel's not too far away. I'll be fine."

"Then you won't mind if I follow behind your car to make sure you're safe." The compromise comes naturally when I'm not the kind of man to back down.

Ever.

It's a strange concept that can only be explained by the unexpected need in my chest to agree to anything Addie wants.

Not to the point where I'm willing to neglect her safety, but at least enough to give her a semblance of control.

"But first, why don't you tell me what's bothering you? You're more antsy than a kid on Christmas morning."

Immediately, she stills. Her wide eyes blink behind her glasses, the frames sliding down her nose again so she has to push them back up in that adorable way I'm starting to find addicting.

What the actual hell?

A forty-two-year-old man shouldn't be turned on by a woman adjusting her glasses. It's an innocent gesture. Commonplace. But nothing about Addie seems commonplace to me.

And that's a problem.

"Oh... It's... I... Are you married?" She bites her lip before squeezing her eyes shut and letting loose a groan of embarrassment at the outburst. One eye peeks open to gauge my reaction.

Fuck, why does she have to be so sweet?

"No, I'm not married. No wife. No girlfriend." My past hasn't been conducive to relationships. Scratching under the brim of my cowboy hat, I suppose my present isn't conducive to them either.

Her shoulders relax under her jacket. "That's good. Well, not good, you know, if you're looking for love or... whatever... I was worried someone might be waiting for you back at the dance, and I've taken up too much of your time and..." She slams a hand over her mouth as if that will stop her sudden rambling.

"I don't know why I said all that," Addie mumbles, messing with the jacket zipper under her chin.

"It's alright." I chuckle and carefully lower her to the ground with my hands wrapped tight around her hips. "I'm just glad we sorted out the potential marriage problem. Unless you...?"

She sure as hell better not be some other man's wife.

Why? Not like she'll ever be yours.

"Me?" The cutest giggle rings through the air, and I swear my dick swells another few inches, which is saying something since the imprint of my zipper is already embedded on the damn thing.

"No, I'm not married."

Would you like to be?

That's it. I've got to get Addie to her hotel before I humiliate myself in front of the poor woman by offering myself as a potential husband.

You're too fucking old for a sweet little thing like her.

Your future is one stranger's decision away from crumbling to ash.

Those are the mantras I repeat as I walk Addie to her car and trail behind her sedan with my truck before waving good-bye once she's safely inside the hotel lobby. They almost drown out the regretful mourning of not asking for her number.

Almost.

IN THE MORNING, I WAKE up surly and fatigued. Amazing what a night of tossing and turning with frustration will get you.

"You okay?" Samuel, my best friend and owner of the ranch next to ours, shovels another mound of trampled hay and horseshit out of the stall next to me. He came over this morning to complain about the rich city guys who bought the land abutting his and who now want to purchase his ranch, too.

I grunt, reveling in the soreness seeping into my muscles from pushing too hard for too long. Maybe I'll wear myself out so badly that sleep won't be a stranger tonight.

After listening to his grievances with wealthy businessmen picking Montana as their newest playground, and commiserating with his plight considering my own experience with bored CEOs, I roped him into helping me muck stalls.

"Do I need to accidentally miss the wheelbarrow and toss this shit over your head for a response? Grunting like a caveman doesn't cut it."

I pause my shoveling and glare through the metal bars separating us. "Do it, and that manure will be fertilizing your grave in the back forty."

Samuel laughs and continues his work—wisely keeping anything resembling shit on his side of the stable. "He speaks! I was wondering when you'd break. Are you ready to tell me what crawled up your ass and died? Was the dance that bad? I warned you not to go."

"It was fine." I'm prepared for him to keep badgering me for a real answer, but the crunch of gravel reaches my ears. "Someone's coming up the drive. I'll be right back."

A sleek Mercedes parks in front of the main house, and I immediately recognize it as Wilson Tan's vehicle, the executor of Mr. Foster's will. Next to him is a familiar sedan. Silver with a dent on the back bumper.

It can't be.

There must be thousands of silver cars driving around Montana. Just because this particular car looks like the one I followed last night—the one belonging to Adeline—doesn't mean it actually *is* hers.

But that belief is short-lived when she joins Tan, her quilted jacket zipped tight and glasses quickly adjusted, and they approach the steps leading to a wraparound porch, both of them huddled against the harsh wind that decided to grace us this morning.

By the time I enter the house, Samantha has them seated in the living room with steaming cups of coffee in hand.

"Heath, I was just about to text you. Mr. Tan arrived with the first inheritor. Ms. Adeline Croup." Samantha's smile is strained, her eyes conveying shock and anxiety.

We knew this day was coming. When the first heir to Foster's fortune would swoop in and claim the ranch. But we didn't expect to be ambushed.

No warning. No call from Tan. Just him introducing Serenity Ranch's new owner like it's not a monumental moment for us.

In more ways than one.

Because the person receiving my family's legacy—the stranger inheriting our home, becoming our boss—is none other than the woman who kept me up most of last night with dreams of what could've been.

Of kissing and caressing every inch of her curvy body.

Forget our age difference. That's the least of my worries now.

Because Adeline Croup, the sweet and innocent girl of my fantasies, stole my home right out from under me... and ripped my heart out in the process.

CHAPTER SIX

ADELINE

"He's not the best at expressing his emotions beyond a grunt and a scowl."

I OWN A RANCH.

Not just any ranch either.

I own the land Heath's family has worked for generations, and he's none too happy about it if the scowl on his face is anything to go by.

"A heads up would've been appreciated," he grumbles, going to stand behind his sister's chair and resting a hand on her shoulder.

"I apologize for the inconvenience." Mr. Tan doesn't sound very sorry, though. I get the impression that he's itching to escape Guardian Valley and return to his home office in Los Angeles. Unfortunately, he's required to be present as each heir settles on the ranch, then he's free to flee this 'one-horse town'.

His words not mine.

The irony is Guardian Valley is the largest town in the area. I'd hate to hear his thoughts on poor little Alberton or Drexel.

"As Ms. Croup is the first to arrive at Serenity Ranch, she will receive the deed to the land, animals, and structures on the property." He went over all of this when we met in his office yesterday afternoon, but its effect on my nerves is no less impacted from hearing it again.

What the heck was Mr. Foster thinking bequeathing a freaking ranch to the first person to arrive in Guardian Valley? And to keep it a secret, too.

I don't know anything about running a ranch. I'm a city girl. I've never ridden a horse. Never even been on a vacation outside the city limits.

If I'd known about this stipulation of the will, I would've taken my time moving. Asked Mr. Tan to notify me when someone else got the prize of an entire ranching enterprise.

Because, surely, there's someone more qualified than me amongst the other heirs.

They're all strangers.

We met briefly as children after the plane crash. During press conferences and the ensuing lawsuit that ultimately failed due to Mr. Foster's lawyers finding a loophole which alleviated them of responsibility for damages. But that's it.

I never stayed in contact with anyone after the judge dismissed our case.

One of them could be perfect for this job, but instead the livelihoods of Heath and his sister Samantha, along with the other ranch hands and animals, weigh on my shoulders.

"Congratulations," Samantha says. "You must be thrilled."

Thrilled isn't exactly how I'd put it. Especially not with Heath's blue eyes boring into me. I squirm in my seat, hot under his piercing gaze and the thick woolen sweater I donned this morning.

This farce would almost be funny if it didn't make me want to cry. Because, of course, the first man to snag my attention—a ridiculously attractive man who I somehow managed to say more than two words to—now hates me.

After another five minutes, Mr. Tan excuses himself, leaving me alone with Heath and Samantha.

"Why don't I give you a tour of the house? Then—" The screen door slams shut behind Heath's broad back. He stalks toward Mr. Tan, sunlight catching the silver strands threading his hair, but we can't make out what's being said from here. "Don't mind my brother. He's been grumpy since he got back home. *A month ago.*"

Samantha rolls her eyes and motions for me to follow her.

"A month ago? I thought this was your family home before Mr. Foster bought it."

She leads me through a large kitchen filled with white cabinets and the smell of maple syrup, most likely leftover from breakfast.

"It is. Or *was.* Sorry." She shrugs in resignation, and I feel bad all over again. *It's not like you planned to steal her family's ranch.* It was a done deal long before I arrived once Mr. Foster signed the papers.

We walk through the main level where an office and bathroom reside next to the open concept living area before we head upstairs to find four bedrooms.

"This is my room, but I can move to one of the cabins if you're not comfortable sharing the house. I'll still handle cooking for the staff and housekeeping, too, if that's alright with you. Mr. Tan said everything could continue running as-is unless the new owner had different plans."

"Nope," I quickly reassure her. "I'm fine with whatever works best for everyone. You're the expert here, not me. I'm just sorry for the entire situation."

"It's not your fault," Samantha echoes my earlier thoughts. "Truthfully, Mr. Foster saved our asses by purchasing the ranch. Our dad was stubborn and didn't make the necessary changes to keep the business profitable, so while it sucks that we don't own Serenity Ranch anymore, at least it lives on, and we're allowed to live and work here still."

"Of course! I would never kick you or your brother out. It's your home, even if my name's on the deed now."

"I appreciate that, and Heath will, too, once he loses that chip on his shoulder." She leans against the doorjamb and sighs. "He retired from the Marines intent on returning home to run this place, until Dad surprised him by already selling it off. Heath was pissed."

Samantha chuckles. "I wasn't exactly happy about it either, but he took it harder. Then Dad died, and it's been a lot for him to handle. Don't get me wrong, my brother's stronger than most... I mean, you saw the behemoth," her arms spread wide to imitate the breadth of Heath's size, "But he's not the best at expressing his emotions beyond a grunt and a scowl, as you witnessed earlier."

I'm not sure she's giving her brother enough credit, but what do I know? I'm just the woman who fell into his arms last night. Sure, he was friendly. And charming. Teasing. The opposite of the grumpy bear Samantha described. But that was before he knew who I was.

"I understand, and I don't blame him for his reaction. When Mr. Tan arranged for us to meet at the ranch today, it never occurred to me that he wouldn't notify you guys first. Anyone would've been annoyed with the circumstances."

"You're sweet. Too forgiving, but sweet." Samantha squeezes my arm as she passes by to lead me to the master bedroom at the end of the hall. "This one's yours. The bedding has been washed, but you'll probably want to redecorate since this was our dad's room, and it's a little..."

"Rustic?" I supply, eyeing the mounted animal heads scattered along the walls. Those definitely have to go. I can't sleep with Bambi's dead mother staring down at me.

"Like I said, too forgiving. I was going to say *ghoulish*."

"That fits, too."

The sound of horses whinnying outside draws my attention, and I hover near the window, spying Heath's muscular frame by the barn. Dark denim hugs his thick thighs before nipping in at his waist, where a gray chambray shirt is tucked in underneath his heavy coat. Another cowboy hat has found its way on his head and casts shadows over his face.

"Ready for the property tour? Heath knows the land best, but if you'd prefer me to show you around, I can."

"No, I don't want to interrupt your day anymore than I already have." And I don't want an audience for the showdown between me and Heath.

Like we're in the climax of a Western movie and about to duel for land rights.

Yeah, right. I chastise myself for the absurd notion. I'm not a fighter, and Heath's not going to run me off the property. *I think.*

After waving good-bye to Samantha, I cross the gravel path between the house and stables, heading toward the last place I saw Heath. Cabins lay spread out down the way and further beyond them stand craggy mountains, a heavy forest of trees blanketing the landscape in green.

There's no denying the rugged beauty of my new home. Montana is a world away from Missouri. Sure, we have our fair share of rolling hills and natural springs, but they don't compare to the majestic view of Big Sky country.

A man rolls a wheelbarrow out of the open barn doors but stops when he sees me. Setting the load down, he pulls off his gloves before approaching with a dimpled smile.

"The name's Levi," he thrusts a bare hand forward, "Did you make a wrong turn or something? We rarely get pretty ladies like yourself on the ranch."

I blush at his brazen perusal as he holds my hand for a second longer than necessary. That's the second time in two days that a man has complimented me. Maybe I should've moved to Montana years ago.

"Adeline. I'm looking for—"

"Get your fucking hands off her, Cartwright!" The angry bellow scares the bejesus out of me as I jerk backward, stumbling when the heel of my boot slides on a loose patch of gravel.

Levi reaches out to grab my wrist and halt the trajectory of my body slamming into the ground—again—but Heath appears and shoves him aside, tugging me into his arms instead.

"H... Heath?" I tremble in the presence of his obvious fury. Perhaps Samantha had it right, after all. Because the cloudy expression tightening Heath's bearded cheeks is full-on growly. Pissed.

"Go check the fence posts on the east flank," he orders Levi before dragging me into the musty shadows of the barn. Clearly, he doesn't want witnesses to this confrontation either.

Swallowing hard, fear rolls around in my gut. I'm not afraid Heath will hurt me, even now his hold on me remains careful rather than bruising, but I'm scared to see the flirty charm of yesterday transform into hatred.

"I... I didn't know about the ranch. About owning it, I mean," I ramble. "Or that it was your family's. I... I... wasn't hiding it from you last night."

"I know." He stops us in a—*tack room?*— where various bridles, brushes, and other ranch objects are organized along the walls.

"Oh."

His palm smooths over my cheek like it did last night, and the familiar gesture soothes some of my nerves. Surely he's not about to stomp and yell when his touch is so gentle.

"I'm not mad at you," he says, tilting my chin up so our gazes meet in the quiet room.

"Oh." What am I, a freaking puppet? Only capable of expelling one measly sound? *Oh?* But my mind's struggling to adjust to the sudden one-eighty in Heath's demeanor.

"I didn't like seeing Levi's hands on you."

"He was just being friendly, and it was just one hand." I hold up a finger as if he's a three-year old who needs a reminder of how much one equals.

"Doesn't matter. That's one too many." His nostrils flare with a ragged breath, and the rapid beating of his heart is obvious from the throbbing vein in his neck. He's worked up over Levi?

Not me owning the ranch?

Confusion washes away my anxiety. This is when past experience with men would come in handy because I'm having a hard time reading Heath's mood.

If I were to go off of the romance novels and movies I've seen, I'd think he was acting jealous, but that doesn't make sense. Sure, we shared a moment—or something—outside the community center, but nothing that would warrant territorial feelings.

So I must be reading him wrong.

Except his head swoops down, and before I have time to freak out, Heath's mouth is claiming mine with shocking thoroughness. His beard scratches at my skin as he angles his head for a better fit, his grip on my chin tightening.

My hands dangle at my sides, unsure of what to do. This is my first kiss. At freaking twenty-nine years old. And I'm frozen with indecision.

Do I grab his waist? Wrap my arms around his neck? *Oh my gosh, did my glasses just poke him in the eye?*

"Easy, baby," he murmurs, tenderly readjusting my glasses before dropping a smattering of kisses over my lips. "I can feel you thinking from here."

"I... I'm not sure... what to do," I admit. Movies make it look so simple. Virgin heroine lands the man of her dreams as the credits start to roll? No problem, let's kiss like we've done this a million times and fade to black.

In real life, that's definitely not the case. At least not for me. Heath's experienced, mature. He's traveled the world and probably kissed a woman on every continent, and that's not a knock on his past. I'm just stating facts.

I don't want to disappoint him.

"Do whatever you want. Whatever feels good." He lifts one of my hands, presses a kiss to the palm, then places it on his chest. "How about this? How does this feel?"

My fingers bend and release like a cat kneading its paws. Heath's chest is firm and warm—a sturdy spot to rest my hand or my head whenever I need comfort.

"G... good," I whisper. Clearing my throat, I peek up at him through my lashes. "It feels good."

CHAPTER SEVEN

HEATH

"...she's too young, she's my boss. In other words, off-limits for a grizzled old veteran-turned-rancher."

SATISFACTION EASES the tightness in my chest. I was worried Addie would push me away after the rough way I hauled her through the yard and into the stables. My emotions unchecked once I caught sight of her and Levi together—the younger ranch hand clearly flirting with Addie.

Jealousy like I never felt before hit me like a bucking bronco. Forget how pissed I was at Tan for dropping by unannounced. Forget the tangle of emotions seeing Addie again caused. Only one thought materialized in my brain at that moment: *Get Levi the fuck away from my girl.*

Irrational? Hell yes. But did I regret exiling him to the eastern part of the property for the foreseeable future? *Hell no.*

Especially when it means I'm free to kiss Addie's cherry-colored lips and verify she's just as sweet as I imagined.

Nuzzling behind her ear, I place a soft kiss on the delicate skin. "Fate's a funny thing. I was cursing myself last night for not getting your number, and now here you are, the owner of my family's ranch."

"I'm sorry."

"Don't apologize, sweet girl. I know none of this was in your control." And I do. She's not the one I'm angry at for how my life's shaken out.

Dad is. Mr. Foster is. Even Mr. Tan.

But never Adeline.

She shudders as I nibble along her jawline, enjoying the freedom she's giving me. I told myself to leave her alone after I stomped out of the house. Told myself that she's too young, she's my boss. In other words, off-limits for a grizzled old veteran-turned-rancher.

But I lied.

No matter how many times I try to convince myself that a relationship between us isn't a good idea, it doesn't seem to penetrate my thick skull. The only thing registering in my mind is the softness of Addie's curves pressed to my body and the comforting smell of vanilla wafting from her hair.

Even the oversized knitted sweater she's wearing isn't enough to dampen my need. If anything, it heightens my craving to explore all her hidden secrets.

"I don't blame you if you're mad at me. I'm clueless when it comes to running a ranch, which doesn't exactly bode well for you or your sister. Or Levi and whoever else works here."

The mention of Levi causes me to grit my teeth. *Focus.* He's not the one Addie's letting hold and kiss her right now.

"We'll help you. For better or for worse, we'll be by your side."

"You just quoted w... wedding v... vows," she stutters. "Not sure that's in your official job description."

"No..." An idea forms. A crazy solution to all of our problems. "But it could be."

Addie's brown eyes crinkle at the edges behind her glasses. She clears her throat and peers up at me. All innocence and sweet vulnerability. "What are you talking about?"

"We could get married."

Her pretty mouth opens and closes as she processes what I just said. "M... married? You and m... me?"

Nodding, I warm to the arrangement, thinking it through. "It would solve our issue. You need help running the ranch. A ranch you feel guilty about owning in the first place, right?"

A small shake of her head in agreement.

"And I want my family's land back. I want to continue our legacy. With my own children." Bringing up kids so early is probably a death sentence to whatever goodwill I'd garnered for the union so far, but to my surprise, Addie brightens at the possibility.

"Children?" Banked hope hides in the slight tip of a smile and the instinctive clenching of her hand on my chest.

"However many you want. Marry me, baby, and I'll fill that little pussy of yours until you're overflowing with my seed, then I'll fuck you again for good measure."

Addie gasps right before I steal another kiss. Let her think about those words as I prove I'll satisfy every need of hers—starting with a precursor to those babies she wants.

IT'S BEEN TWO DAYS since I issued my promise to breed Serenity Ranch's curvy new owner. Two days since I took over for Billy who was preparing to drive a horse down to Missoula and spend the night before returning.

Addie asked for time to think the proposal over after we regretfully ended our steamy makeout session in the barn.

I agreed to her wishes, but I also knew if I stayed on the property I wouldn't be able to stop myself from crawling into her bedroom window and demanding an answer. Or persuading an answer out of her by fucking her with my tongue.

So, I buckled into the work truck and hauled the trailer down the interstate, keeping to the speed limit and distracting myself by reciting *The Rifleman's Creed*. We learned it in basic training when an obsessed drill instructor pounded it into our memories, but I haven't thought about it in two fucking decades.

Strange what unknowingly lives in our brains until the exact moment the knowledge becomes necessary.

I stayed in a hotel last night then waited until early evening today before driving back home. My patience has reached its end, and I plan on marching into the main house, finding Addie, and coaxing a *yes* out of her by any means necessary.

But when I enter the house, applause blares from the television as Addie's voice rings out every so often.

"Who is Elizabeth Barrett Browning?" she asks, and I wonder who she's speaking to because Samantha is gone helping her friend at the bakery prepare for a birthday party.

"Yes!"

Peering around the doorway, I spy Addie on the couch with an open laptop next to her and a notebook in her lap. She scratches something on the paper before returning her attention to the television screen.

"This 3-letter word can refer to a state of intoxication, making a person incandescent," the game show host says.

"What is lit?"

A contestant answers correctly a second after Addie, and she bends her head to write something else in her notebook.

Fuck me. She's keeping track of her score. She's sitting there cross-legged in another knit sweater with her hair in a messy bun and playing along to Jeopardy! on TV.

This woman is literally trying to kill me with how fucking adorable she is.

I need to make her mine.

My wife.

CHAPTER EIGHT

ADELINE

"I can't get enough of you, sweet girl."

I TALLY MY TOTAL SCORE after the final Jeopardy! clue answer is revealed and shrug in annoyance. This is one area where I allow myself to 'risk it all' but today did not go in my favor. $3600 down to $0.

Oh well, maybe I'll have better luck tomorrow.

"How'd you do?" The curious voice surprises me, and my head jerks to the right to find Heath propped against the door jamb. His arms are crossed over his chest. His booted feet crossed as well.

How did I not know he's been here watching me this entire time?

He's too attractive for my own good, and he wants to marry *me.*

"T... tied for last place, not my best work." *This man wants to be my husband.* It's the only thing rattling around in my brain now, so I continue to ramble, afraid that maybe I imagined the whole thing.

"I prefer to win. Though I also prefer the episodes when Alex Trebek was still the host. I'm sad that we lost him. He seemed like a good guy—"

"Have you thought about my question?" His question cuts off my blathering, and I gulp a lungful of air in relief.

He eases into the living room and bends down on one knee like he really is proposing with a ring and all.

Guess it wasn't my imagination.

Which is why it's all I've been thinking about since yesterday. Even during the game, my mind was subconsciously working out what I should do.

Well, that's not true. I know what I want to do.

I want to marry Heath. He's offering me everything I've ever wanted. A husband, kids, family. But is it right to marry him just because a dead billionaire gave me his family's property?

I don't know.

If it's what he wants.

"What's it going to be, baby?" he asks, gently removing the pen from my hand to set it aside.

There's a softness in his gaze. Maybe if there was an ounce of regret, of concern over me agreeing to his crazy proposition, I'd be able to turn him down.

But there's not.

There's only confident hope.

So I give him what he wants. What *I* want.

"Yes, I'll marry you."

"That's my girl." He smiles before it gets lost in a passionate kiss to seal the deal. Heath guides me backward onto the couch, his large body covering mine after carefully removing my laptop.

I groan at the solid weight of him pressing me into the soft cushions. Unlike our last kiss, I immediately wrap my arms around his neck to pull him closer. I'm not going to mess this up.

Heath's warm palm slides under my sweater to cup my breast. The heat of his touch makes me shiver, and I arch into his embrace.

"Greedy, aren't you? Don't worry, I'll take care of you. My sweet little Addie." Heath quickly rips my sweater overhead, leaving me exposed in just my bra. It's plain beige, but he doesn't seem to mind, growling at the sight.

With a quick snap of his fingers, the hooks on the front come undone and burst free, my breasts spilling out. I've never been so exposed in my life and part of me feels the need to cover up.

Modest skirts and sweater sets have been my life since I became old enough to wear Gran's hand-me-downs. It used to bother me—dressing frumpy in clothes meant for seniors—until their cozy comfort outweighed my miniscule fashion sense.

Besides, what did it matter what I wore when I barely left the house?

But that was before.

Before my inheritance. Before Heath.

I wish I owned sexy underwear rather than economical cotton neutrals. Maybe then I'd feel like somebody worth looking at with desire.

"God, you're beautiful," Heath murmurs, shaming my insecure thoughts. Clearly, he doesn't have a problem with basic underthings and jiggly breasts and bellies.

He drops his head low and licks around a sensitive nipple before drawing it between his lips to suckle. He alternates back and forth between each breast, each time increasing his roughness until his teeth are nipping at the reddened buds.

"I can't get enough of you, sweet girl." His heated gaze runs up my bare body to meet my stunned expression. The obvious need in his voice. His tensed muscles. The hard bulge nudging between my thighs.

They shock me into silence. It's like I'm essential to Heath. Like if he doesn't have me—*and soon*—then he'll combust.

And heck, maybe I will, too.

Tears prick the backs of my eyes at my good fortune. I'm going to marry this man as soon as he'll have me. And even if he's not marrying me out of love, fragile hope blooms in my heart that we'll eventually get there.

We'll fall in love and live happily ever after.

I don't care how naive it sounds.

Two fingers slide under my waistband to brush aside my panties. "Fuck, you're soaked. You like me sucking on those pretty tits of yours, baby?"

"Y... yes...." I can barely get the word out, but at least it's the appropriate time for one-word answers.

"Good, because I plan on licking and sucking every part of you for a good long time. You're going to wear my marks around this ranch so every man knows you're mine... So every man in Guardian Valley knows you're mine," he corrects.

"Yes... P... please, Heath."

His rough fingertips circle my clit, around and round, before slipping lower and plunging into my wet channel. He continues the rhythm—*circle, circle, plunge*—until I can't take it anymore.

Drawing his face to mine, I press a desperate kiss to his mouth, needing that intimate connection, before gasping for air and shouting my release.

"That's it, Addie. There's my sweet girl. Come for your man. Come for your husband."

I collapse against the couch, drained of energy, and float in post-orgasmic bliss as his commands echo in my mind.

Come for your husband.

I've never heard sweeter words.

CHAPTER NINE

HEATH

"I promised to satisfy her every need."

JUDGE HELLER STAMPS our marriage license and pronounces us *man and wife*. If it were up to me, Addie and I would've married the day after she came on my fingers, announcing her consent to my proposal.

But we agreed it'd be wiser to wait so I could sign a prenup to protect her, since she was coming into an inheritance. The damned slow local lawyer took a day to draw up the contract.

I couldn't care less about Addie's money, but I never want people to question our marriage and motives. Yes, the impetus for our union was ensuring the ranch stayed in my family and to take the burden of running it off Addie's shoulders. But this thing between us went beyond a mere business decision.

"You may kiss the bride, if you'd like."

We may not be in a church with the traditional wedding get-up, but I'm sure as hell going to take every opportunity to kiss my wife.

Addie flushes pink as I wrap my arms around her and dip her back for a heartstopping kiss. We've kept it PG at home since I made her come on the couch. But that shit ends tonight.

I plan on stuffing her full of my cock after tasting her cherry.

"Alright, buddy, let her breathe." Samantha taps my shoulder, though she's smiling when I let Addie up.

My sister cornered me in my cabin after finding out about the engagement and laid into me like a mama bear protecting her cub. It would've been cute how intent she was to come to Addie's defense, but my girl didn't need protection from me.

I'm her protector.

"Congrats, girl. Welcome to the family!" Addie and Samantha hug before we exit the courtroom, allowing the next couple inside.

We arrived towards the end of the lunch hour, and a line of other couples formed during the ten minutes we were with the judge. A photographer snapped pictures of a bride dressed for a magazine cover rather than the courthouse, and I silently vowed that one day Addie would have a chance to wear a proper wedding gown.

Maybe at a vow renewal.

The women chatter on the drive back to the ranch, but as soon as we hit Serenity Ranch property, I hurry to drop Samantha off at the main house before driving on to the cabin Addie and I decided to commandeer.

"I like your place. It reminds me of my Gran's."

That's what she said when I brought up the living arrangements, and I can't say I'm unhappy with her decision. The big house has always been Samantha's territory. I haven't lived there full-time since I was eighteen—over twenty fucking years ago—so claiming a cabin with Addie and making it our home sounds perfect.

We still need to unload the bulk of Addie's belongings once the transport company she hired arrives with a pod full of furniture, so until then she's making do living out of a suitcase.

After sweeping her over the threshold like a proper bride, I let her head upstairs to the master bedroom first, willing myself to give her a moment of privacy. But my resolve weakens within minutes, and I quickly follow her upstairs.

Addie doesn't need to primp, pluck, or *anything* for tonight. She's beautiful as she is, and that's who I crave as I stop at the bedroom door.

She's by the expansive windows that offer a wide view of the rugged Montana landscape at our doorstep.

A soft, "Heath?," drifts through the air.

"Don't turn around." I command, going to stand behind her as we both stare out the bedroom window to the miles of land beyond. My hands coast down her sides while my mouth hovers next to her ear. "It's not everyday a man marries a gorgeous woman... What should I do with you, wife?"

She leans back into me, allowing me to take her weight as she replies, "L... love me." The vulnerable admission wraps around my heart and squeezes tight.

With a pained groan, I swiftly divest her from the pink cardigan and blouse she'd chosen for the marriage ceremony and fling her bra to the floor.

My hands drift upward until they cup her bare breasts, thumbs circling her areolas. Addie's audible breaths increase with the evidence of her arousal. "Heath..."

A filthy idea flits through my mind and unable to deny myself, I whisper, "Such a pretty picture my wife makes pleading for her husband. I think it's time you show me what you need."

My teeth nip her neck as the suggestiveness of my words sink in. Addie releases a brief sound of confusion before I order, "Lift your skirt, baby, and show me how you please yourself. I'd help, but my hands are currently full with these luscious tits." I tweak her nipples in reminder.

"I'm not sure..." A note of fear tinges her voice.

"Obey your husband," I say firmly, then gentler, "No one can see us. It's just acres of land outside, and you and me here—husband and wife."

Slowly, Addie pulls the long skirt higher up her thighs. The trust shown in the move heightens my arousal. Her trust is important to me, and I never want to abuse it.

White panties reflect in the window as she carefully slips underneath the cotton and lets her fingers inch inside. The moment Addie touches her clit, she gasps and leans further into my arms.

"That's right, sweet girl." I praise her with murmured words of encouragement as she begins a rhythmic stroking. Her soft moans of pleasure vibrate through my body, settling in my cock.

I play with her nipples, pinching and pulling then delicately brushing them back and forth. "You're doing so well. Petting your pretty pussy for your husband." My head dips to lick away the sweat forming on her shoulder, reveling in the salty essence.

"Heath... Oh!"

Suddenly, a shudder wracks her limbs, back arching into the waves of her orgasm until, replete, Addie sags against me. I gentle my movements, rubbing along every inch of exposed skin to bring her back to Earth.

"Give me your hand." The words are husky as I force them past my dry throat. She lifts one hand, and I smile at her naivete. "No, baby, your other hand."

Twisting to look up at me, her brows furrow at the request, but eventually Addie obeys. Bringing her hand to my lips, I let her watch as I suck her fingers clean of her cream. Banked heat unfurls in her eyes as unspoken needs travel between us.

"I don't think I'm quite satisfied yet." I remove my blazer then unbutton part of my shirt. Suitably comfortable, I retreat to the bed and lay down in the center before motioning Addie forward. "Place your thighs around my shoulders. I need to taste that sweet cherry of yours directly from the source."

"Heath, I don't think..."

"Don't think... Come here." I'm enjoying this cat and mouse game of pushing Addie past her limits. She's so reserved—shy—but I know she needs this release just as much as I need to give it to her.

Addie hesitantly gathers her skirt and shuffles closer. The mattress dips as she puts one knee then the other on the comforter before shifting to straddle me.

"There's my good girl."

A red blush floods to the top of her skin. My wife definitely likes being told how sweet and perfect she is. And I plan on telling her as often as I can.

Wrapping my arms beneath her legs, I hike her higher up my chest, so the wet heat of her pussy hovers above my mouth. My hunger for her taste intensifies as I stiffen in anticipation. I press a soft kiss to the inside of her trembling thigh in an effort to comfort her, then glide closer to her curls, the fading sunlight glinting off the drops of wetness clinging to them.

Her sweet flavor coats my tongue as it swipes through her folds, searching for the place where her pleasure centers. Finding the engorged button, I playfully tease the sensitive flesh, and Addie releases a frustrated growl.

It's fucking adorable, and so out of character for her to voice her displeasure. Addie's not a doormat, but she's young and innocent, preferring to roll with life's punches rather than cause conflict.

She brings herself more firmly against my mouth, and a brief chuckle at her eagerness rumbles in my throat. How quickly she surrenders herself to me.

Letting Addie dictate the pace, we soon find a pleasing motion of her rocking against my mouth, riding my tongue like a champion cowgirl.

"Yes... please... I'm so close..." Her movements grow more choppy, less coordinated, before a rush of cream signals her release. I happily clean her up as best I can with my mouth before Addie lazily slides down my body to rest her head against my shoulder.

Satisfaction lies thick in the air—hers and mine.

Pausing at the thought, I realized I'd been so focused on Addie, I hardly noticed my own release at her pleasure, the cum seeping through my slacks making itself known. Taken aback at the loss of control, I contemplate the woman in my arms.

My wife.

Right from the start, she managed to break through my barriers and bring out a whole new level of intimacy that I was unaware even existed. It was unnerving.

"That was much more than I expected when I thought of my wedding night." Addie's soft words break through my spiraling thoughts. Her hand rests on my chest, occasionally tugging on the short curls there.

"Was it?" I stroke her temple, brushing little wisps of hair back from her face.

There's a sound of assent before she adds, "But what about you? You didn't..." She makes a vague gesture to below my waist.

"I did," I admit, disconcerted again at the surprise act. "Your pleasure brought me mine."

"Oh." A note of satisfaction infuses the one word.

Clearly, the admission isn't unwelcome, and I can't fault her. What couple didn't want a mutually gratifying sexual relationship?

But the night isn't over yet.

Addie might be satisfied with making me come in my pants like a fucking teen, but I'm not. I promised her babies. I promised to satisfy her every need.

That's exactly what I'm going to do—with my cock deep in her hot virgin cunt.

CHAPTER TEN

ADELINE

"I'm still shy around Heath yet also braver than I've ever been in my entire life."

HEATH SHIFTS BENEATH me, and I tilt my head up, suddenly aware of my weight. "Am I getting too heavy for you?"

"Hardly." He tenderly rolls us over so I'm pinned to the mattress by his muscular form. "I'm ready to finally claim you with my cock now that you're all soft and pliant." A possessive gleam appears in his eyes as the tip of his cock nudges between my thighs to rest at the clenching entrance of my pussy.

"O... okay." Nice to know my way with words hasn't changed with the life-altering experience of riding a man's face. There's a strange dichotomy within me—one where I'm still shy around Heath yet also braver than I've ever been in my entire life.

Neither of us move.

A mutual reluctance to break the dreamy moment of anticipation passing between us.

Until Heath growls and thrusts forward with measured strokes. His eyes never leave mine as he gauges my reactions. If I flinch, he pauses. If I sigh, he continues.

It's sweet agony before he's buried deep, and we're chest to chest, the smattering of silver-flecked hair tickling my breasts.

"I swear you're trying to kill me with this tight cunt," Heath grumbles, grinding his pelvis against my clit before sliding back and plunging forward again. "You're fucking made for me, aren't you, sweet girl? A curvy little beauty just for me. *Fuck!*"

Sweat beads at his temple, and I delicately trace the damp sheen into his short-cropped hair. His words have me unconsciously clamping down on his cock, emboldened by the power I feel at driving this controlled rancher to his limit.

"Just... for you..." I agree. The truth of it settles in my bones. For years, it was just me, Gran, and a host of her friends from the senior center. Now, I have Heath and his sister. They're my family now, thanks to Mr. Foster.

"Damn right." Heath grips the back of my thigh to adjust the angle of his strokes. Soon we're both panting with need, racing to the finish line, as the tension shatters, shared groans of satisfaction filling the air.

We lay in a tangle on the bed, our heartbeats thundering together in a matching rhythm.

"Are you okay?"

"N... never been better." And that's the God-honest truth.

EPILOGUE ONE

HEATH

"All you need to worry about is keeping you and our baby safe and healthy."

"DAMN, GIRL, YOU'RE fucking glowing." Jasmine winks as Samantha shudders and groans, her eyes pinching closed.

"Ugh, I don't want to hear why! Y'all are cute, and I'm happy for you two, but I do not need the dirty details."

"Speak for yourself." Jasmine rolls out more cookie dough to cut out shapes for the party tomorrow night. She owns the local bakery and has welcomed Addie into the Guardian Valley fold like my wife was born and raised here.

Deciding to save my sister from hearing about Addie and I's sexual exploits, I step into the kitchen and immediately wrap my arms around Addie's expanding waist.

I promised my wife babies, and that's what she's getting—starting with the one resting safe in her belly. She's five months along, so we figured we should have a belated celebratory wedding reception combined with a baby shower, which is why the main house's kitchen looks like a dervish made of flour and sugar just rolled through.

"Hey, Samantha, have you been up to the old hunter's cabin lately?" The question is why I'm interrupting their fun in the first place. Levi mentioned seeing lights on at the vacant cabin the other day.

"No. Why?"

"Levi thought he saw activity up there. But maybe it was sunlight reflecting off the windows or something. I'll ride up there soon to check things out." The journey could be hiked within an hour, but why waste time strolling through the mountains when a horse could get me there and back quicker?

Especially when I have a pregnant wife waiting for me at home.

"I hope everything's alright..." Addie bites her lip, her nose scrunching to readjust her glasses since her hands are covered in flour.

After fixing them for her, I kiss her temple. "Whatever it is, it shouldn't concern you. All you need to worry about is keeping you and our baby safe and healthy. I'll take care of the rest."

"Aww... that's sweet," Jasmine says while Samantha pretends to gag.

Addie and I share a smile. Our relationship might have started out unconventionally, but it's no less stronger because of it.

The day I learned my family's legacy had been sold out from under me, I'd been pissed. Bitter with the world. But it turned out to be the best thing to ever happen to me because it brought Adeline into my life.

My sweet wife.

She hasn't had it easy since losing her mom then Gran. The way she described it, she lived in a bubble for most of her life before moving to Guardian Valley.

We both needed the shake-up Foster provided when he decided to bequeath his fortune along with this ranch to five strangers. I'm just glad one of them turned out to be the love of my life.

Wonder what that means for the other four...

What's going on up in that secluded cabin? Find out in Samantha's story next, *Montana Warrior*! Turn the page for a sneak peek at the first chapter!

CHAPTER ONE

SAMANTHA MANNING

"I know most of the men in Guardian Valley, and no one, I mean no one, meets the description of this freaking lumberjack."

THIS IS A STUPID IDEA. A stupid, reckless idea. But it's too late to turn back now. Too late to let my brother—a former Marine—handle whatever awaits me at the top of this damn mountain.

Okay, so not quite a mountain, but a freaking big hill. One that I was not prepared to hike this morning after last night's festivities, AKA my brother and sister-in-law's belated wedding reception/baby shower.

But I was still feeling a little sad—a little restless—after watching them dance and laugh and be so freaking adorable together. Who'd have thought my big gruff brother would find love with such a sweet woman like Adeline?

Would fall in love and get married before me? Heath's hopeless romantic little sister?

I sigh as the secluded cabin I'm headed toward comes into view. It's a cute little house settled on a ledge that juts into the river, rushing water running by two sides of it. The sunrises are gorgeous if you happen to be sitting out on the porch at just the right time.

But I haven't been up here in forever. The trek from the main house through the woods has my body huffing and puffing for air.

"Just one peek then turn around," I tell myself.

I don't know what possessed me to choose this as my morning task to shake those pesky insecurities of being alone forever. Heath said it looked like someone had been up here in passing. He definitely didn't mean for me to go check it out.

It's probably a rogue hunter who wandered onto our land—or rather Adeline's land since a dead billionaire CEO bequeathed it to her after our dad sold the ranch. Or maybe a lost hiker, though we probably would've heard about that on the news.

It could be a serial killer for all I knew. A killer on the lam, searching for his next victim. Preferably a brunette with extra curves and no dating prospects.

Time to lay off the true crime docs, girl.

But something was drawing me up here to find out what was going on for myself. Like I said: a stupid, reckless—

The smartest damn thing I've ever done in my life.

The sound of an ax splitting through a log rings through the air, and after cresting a ridge of rocks, I spy a man through the thicket of trees. A giant, really. Drenched in sweat and wielding a giant-ass ax overhead before swinging it down with a grunt.

Holy cow.

My pussy clenches instinctually as my hand falls to the tree trunk in front of me, nails digging into the rough bark.

Who the hell is that?

I know most of the men in Guardian Valley, and no one, I mean *no one*, meets the description of this freaking lumberjack.

Rippling muscles bulge beneath his tan skin. Skin that's covered in ragged scars, bright pink across his back and shoulders. Short blonde hair glints under the sun, and I desperately need him to turn around so I can see his face.

No doubt accompanied by a massive chest heaving with his exertion.

Oh god. Is it possible to come just from watching a hot stranger chop wood? Because the longer I stare, the harder it becomes to breathe and the damper my panties get.

Alright, Samantha, you've got this. How does one approach the living embodiment of every wet dream they've ever had?

Hey, stranger! Mind if I ass you a question?

My eyes skim down his torso to where his jeans rest over his hips and firm butt. Yeah, no, I don't want to creep him out with puns about body parts. Especially body parts I'm ogling from afar like a horny spinster desperate to be tossed over his shoulder and—

Oh, wait... That's exactly what I am.

It's your family's land, or it used to be, or it is again since Heath married Adeline. Honestly, the ownership of the ranch has exchanged hands so much lately, it's a miracle I don't have whiplash.

Either way—Heath's or Adeline's—this stranger has no cause to be here. Chopping down our trees and looking damn good doing it. So, I'm just going to march over there and demand he tell me what the heck he's doing here. There's probably a perfectly logical explanation, and once that's taken care of, we can move on to more pressing matters.

Like the lusty devil currently residing on my shoulder.

"Take a picture, it'll last longer," a male voice calls out, the throwback insult from middle school jarring me out of my spiraling. "And while you're at it, you can get the hell off my land."

His land?

Looks like things are heating up on the mountain…
Find out what happens next in *Montana Warrior*!

THANKS FOR READING & DON'T FORGET TO RATE/ REVIEW!

Please consider leaving a rating/review. Ratings & reviews are the #1 way to support an indie author like me.

The more reviews, the more my books are shown to other potential readers! And they serve as guides to readers on whether or not to take a chance on an indie author.

I appreciate your support!

XO, Hallie

ABOUT THE AUTHOR

Hallie prefers steamy, insta-love stories where curvy girls are claimed by filthy-talking heroes. And when she ran out of reading material, she decided to write her own stories. If you want a quick, hot read, she's your girl!

Find more about Hallie Bennett HERE[1]!